DIRTY BIKERS

Steamy BWWM Mafia

Leandra Camilli

CONTENTS

CHAPTER 1

When I opened my eyes and found out that I was in the arms of a burly, bearded man, I almost screamed. His arms were heavy, confident, and he was holding me like I weighed nothing. I could feel waves of heat coming out of his body, and it was intoxicating.

His face wasn't neat and it showed his age, and he wasn't even aware that I was already awake. I never thought that I would wake up and find myself in his arms.

I thought that I was studying in my room, immersed in what I was reading, and trying to solve a difficult problem that was taking me weeks just to make some advancements in it.

And then, I couldn't remember anything after that. All I could remember was that there was blackness in my vision soon after that.

And now I was in the arms of this man, who looked dangerously like a biker. I could even see the patch on his chest, and it said that he was a member of The Lone Devils.

They were some of the most well-respected and frightening biker groups in the state.

I shuddered, wondering what it was that he was planning to do to me. Looking around me, I noticed that I was outside my apartment. I could see some smoke going up and what appeared to be a reddish, bright light in the background, right where my apartment was supposed to be, but no more than that.

I was a little dizzy, but other than that, I was fine and I could process what was happening around me. I wasn't weak and I could fight back against this biker if I wanted to, but I wasn't doing it because something about him was showing me that he wasn't going to hurt me.

I didn't know his name, but I could see the other patch on his chest and it said that his nickname was Forger. I was going to keep that in mind, I thought.

There was no way that this wasn't going to end with us talking at least for a little while at some point.

I could tell that he was much older than me. He took care of himself and kept himself in shape. I didn't think that he was the kind of man who put on makeup, but it wasn't like he needed it, anyway. His face was good the way it was, and I felt that if he put on any makeup, it would only ruin it.

I didn't know where he was taking me, but he appeared to be determined about it.

His jacket was trendy, it looked like it was made of high-quality materials, though also that it was a little old. I would never say that to him, knowing the consequences of that, even though I wanted to.

When I thought that this was going to keep on going forever, he looked down and finally noticed that I was awake.

"Didn't realize that you were already awake," the biker said and then he added, "want to tell me what your name is?"

"Maybe you should start by explaining yourself. Why am I in your arms, and where are you taking me?"

"You really don't remember anything, Buttercup?" He asked, his fingers moving around my neck and making me feel goosebumps all over my body. There was no denying he knew what he was doing, and how dominating he was.

Not to mention the way he brushed his fingers around my neck... He knew that he was hitting every right spot in me, and that he was making me slightly wet, just thinking about what we could do together.

I shook my head. It was just so good to be in his arms that I wasn't even struggling against that. If anything, this was what I always wanted to do one day.

Forger was turning one of my dreams real, and I couldn't even say that to him. I didn't think that doing so was wise.

"I remember that I was studying in my room."

"Well, there was a huge explosion and I had to go there to save you."

I narrowed my eyes slightly.

"Are you telling me the truth?" I asked and he chuckled.

"Of course I'm telling you the truth. Why do you think I would be lying right now, and about something like that, too?" He asked and his questions made sense.

"I want to go there and see it for myself," I said and he shook his head.

"No can do, Buttercup. You are hurt, probably feeling a little dizzy after what happened, and I need to take you somewhere where you're going to be safe."

"No, I want to go and see what happened to my apartment. I live there, everything I have is there, including my computer and personal documents. Without them, I'm nothing."

"Where you're going with me, you aren't going to need those things," he explained and his voice was deep and hoarse enough to make me think that he wasn't kidding. If anything, it was the most truthful thing that he said in a while, and I didn't know how to take that.

All I knew was that I was curious about it and that I could go and see what happened to my apartment another time, even though I didn't know when that would be.

"I don't trust you."

"If you don't trust me, then you can just leave."

He was still taking me somewhere that I didn't know anything about, the streets dark and the moon high in the sky.

It wasn't a full moon, far from it, but the shine coming from it was enough to let me make out some of his face, and I didn't need more than that to know that he was more danger than I could handle.

I gulped when he turned around the corner and I craned my head so that I could look at what was ahead of me. A motorcycle was positioned by the end of the alleyway, idle and almost looking like it was resting. And yet, the way that it was almost looking at me was more menacing than any other bike I'd seen in my life.

His bike was different. Made for him, pitch black, with details made of chrome, and shining under the gentle light coming from the moon. The headlight was turned off, but the way that the front of the bike was aimed at me was almost making me think that I wasn't hallucinating when I thought that it was looking at me.

"So, you really aren't going to leave?" He asked, pulling up the side of his lips. He knew that I couldn't just leave, and I wasn't going to. My things in my apartment were important, but it wasn't like they were my entire life.

If anything, I'd already been doing everything in my power so that I didn't have to keep depending on them. I was in the process of getting rid of them, and I never thought that the endpoint of that was going to be the apartment going up in flames.

"I'm not, but if you are lying to me, then you're going to regret it."

He cackled, stopping by the bike and taking a breath.

And then Forger asked, "Are you feeling better now? I need to put you down and then on my bike so that we can leave here. As I said, I'm going to take you where you're going to be safe, where you can have anything you want, and tomorrow, when you're feeling better, you can figure out what to do with your life."

I analyzed his face and studied his proposal. I knew that it was enticing and that it was making me want to go along with it, but the problem was that I was also trying to push myself away from these parts of my life.

I was far too prone to dropping everything that I was building toward just so that I could have a change of life, and I didn't think that going against that was wise.

"Alright, fine. I'm going with you, but only because I have no better choice, and not because I feel that this is the right thing to be doing or something like that."

"You can do whatever you want, but know that you are indeed making the right choice. I'm going to take you to my biker club, where everyone there will treat you fairly and kindly.

You don't need to worry about them. Worry about your bank and if you can make them cover some of the expenses you're going to have to piece your life back together. Or alternatively, you can live with us for the rest of your life."

I chuckled, allowing him to put me on his bike. I wrapped my arms around his body, settled my head on the crook of his neck, and then said, "Like hell I'm going to do that."

CHAPTER 2

Stepping under the showerhead, I looked around and couldn't help but realize that this place wasn't much worse than the apartment where I used to live. There wasn't much here in terms of luxury and I never expected any differently.

I knew that the life of a biker was marred by their poorness, that they were always getting by, and that the place where they lived was filthy, especially in terms of smell.

There was this constant, unforgiving smell of cigars, cheap beer, and other things in the air, and it was almost puke-inducing. Not to mention the pounding music coming from downstairs, the graffiti on the walls, clothing pieces thrown all over the floor, weed stashes on the bed, and a couple of other things that showed me I didn't want to be here.

It was dark outside, I was tired, and the only thing I wanted right now was to finish my shower. I was slightly surprised that there was a shower cubicle and that it was separate from the surrounding environment. It was cleaner than I thought as well, which was another surprise.

It was possible that Forger always came here to clean it. It would be one of the few things that he bothered to keep clean often, I thought.

I closed the door of the shower cubicle, turned on the shower-head, and then adjusted the temperature of the water so that it was lukewarm. The water was sufficient and the temperature was just right. I closed my eyes and let myself be immersed in it, thinking about everything that happened today.

The water was moving down around my body and time was passing. I wasn't washing my body, but I was washing away all the stress that was in my mind. I was getting rid of it and that, in turn, brought a smile to my face.

Was I worried that one of the bikers was going to open the door and come inside the room when I wasn't looking? I was, but I wasn't even thinking about that right now. The only thing I was thinking about was making sure that I wasn't stressed anymore. I didn't want to be any more stressed than I already was.

Minutes later, when I wasn't stressed any longer, I finished washing my body, and then I turned off the showerhead.

I turned around and when I was going to open the door of the shower cubicle, I noticed a shadow on the floor, right outside of it.

For a moment, I panicked. I threw my arms around my body, trying to cover my nipples and pussy. I had no idea who was outside the shower cubicle, but whoever he was, he must've seen me naked. And that was something that terrified me so much it was making my heart pound in my head.

"Who are you?" I asked, hoping that this was nothing more than a hallucination and that I was going to find out that the shadow didn't even exist. But then the seconds passed, he lowered his arms, and then sighed. I knew that I wasn't dreaming any of this and that it was indeed happening.

"It's me, Forger. I came here to check up on you and I was waiting for you to finish your shower. Looks like you are already feeling much better."

I was taken aback by his lack of reaction, almost as if he thought that his intrusion was normal to him. It was possible that it was, but for me things were different, even if I was finding his 'bad boy that doesn't care about anything that isn't himself' attitude hot and charming at the same time.

I could feel my pussy getting slightly wet, and I just hoped that he wasn't going to notice it, even though I was aware he was much smarter than that, and also much more perceptive.

"You shouldn't have come into the room while I was still taking my shower."

"It's my room and I can do anything I want in it. Not to mention that I didn't look at you when I noticed that you were still taking your shower."

"It's still disrespectful. I know that you are a biker and a jerk, but I still thought that you were better than this."

He chuckled, crossing his arms over his chest again.

"I know you want to make me believe that, but things are different than that, aren't they?" He said, taking a deep breath. Even though I couldn't see him, other than his shadow, I could tell that he was getting hard. Or at least, I was imagining that he was. And that thought was hardening my nipples.

"You don't know anything about me."

"Maybe not, but I'm still worried about you. Feeling better now that we're talking?" He asked, pausing. I could still hear his breathing despite the pounding music coming from downstairs. This place was a little nasty, but I didn't expect any different from a biker club.

And I was a little surprised he asked that. More and more, Forger was showing me that there was a true, caring man under his biker persona, and I didn't know how to take that. Knowing that was unsettling me.

"I am and thanks for the shower. I really needed it."

"Look at the bed. I bought you some things I think you're going to like," he said and I obeyed him. I looked at the bed, finding a new shirt, skirt, and a couple of other clothing pieces I could wear. Even though I was far from the bed, I could tell that they were plus size.

They probably fit me, but I didn't know if I was going to wear them. I knew that my clothes were dirty and dusty, but I still didn't want anything else from Forger than the shower and sleeping in the biker club until tomorrow morning.

When it was tomorrow morning, I would get my things and then make some calls, and that would be sufficient. I would find a new place where I could live, buy a different computer, and get copies of my original documents. Everything was going to be fine, I reassured myself.

"You shouldn't have bought me anything. I don't need it."

"Really? I thought you were going to be grateful."

I bit my bottom lip. I didn't want to be an asshole, but everything he was doing was forcing me to be that way. He was forcing me to be strong, to hold my ground, and to say that I wasn't interested. If he was thinking that he was going to get under my skirt, then he was going to be disappointed.

But at the same time, I didn't have any other clothes other than the ones I was wearing after the apartment was burned to a crisp. And yeah, pretty much nothing that was in there was saved, and thus I had to start everything from the beginning.

Even my work from college, which I was going to save in the cloud, was lost.

"Cat got your tongue?" He asked, stepping away from the door suddenly and then walking out of the room. For a moment, I thought that it was a trap, but then I heard his footsteps receding in the hallway, and I knew that meant I was safe and had some privacy, even though it wasn't enough.

After some more minutes, when I felt I could finally be braver again, I opened the door of the shower cubicle and stepped outside. I checked the room just to make sure that no hidden bikers were in there, and then I stepped over to the bed. The clothes were neatly placed on it, almost like he cared about such a detail.

Someone like Forger certainly didn't care about that, but it wasn't like it was even the point of this. The point was that the clothes were actually nice, he bought them for me today, and they smelled nice as well.

They didn't appear to be from a thrift store as well, which was another positive.

I finished drying myself with the towel and then put on the clothes, checking myself out in the mirror. I turned my body from side to side slightly, loving my new look.

Even though I was busting my ass to be richer, the truth was that I was always usually content with cheap things, as long as they looked good, which was the case with these clothes.

It was for that reason I was beginning to feel thankful for the way he appeared to be caring about me, even though I was already promising myself that it wasn't going to change anything.

If anything, I was going to make use of it just so that I could get my foot on the ground and start anew. And then, I'd discard Forger like he was nothing.

CHAPTER 3

"Thinking that you're going out without at least saying that you're thankful about it?" Someone behind me asked right when I was stepping outside the club. I turned around immediately, meeting none other than another biker with his arms crossed over his chest, looking at the ground as if he couldn't even be bothered to look at me.

The way that he was doing that was certainly a little offensive, but I'd dealt with worse. And I was pretty sure that he was aware of that.

"I need to go to the City Hall. There are some things I need to do there."

"Well, you should at least say that you're thankful for the way we've been treating you. We've been keeping you safe this whole time."

"It hasn't been that long, and I didn't ask for your help anyway."

"Ouch. You can hurt more than I thought someone like you could," he said, uncrossing his arms and then finally lifting his head. He looked at me, stepped toward me, and I realized that, just like with Forger, he was much taller than me. But it wasn't like they were similar or anything like that. In fact, they appeared to be much different as bikers.

The guy that was standing in front of me had blond, short hair, fair skin, and no beard on his face. His eyes were jade-green, attentive, and he was looking at me as though he was staring into my soul.

His hair was so blond that I almost couldn't see it on his arms, even though they were supposed to be hairy, like the rest of his body.

I could smell the fragrance of his cologne in the air, and it was filling my lungs and was intoxicating. It was almost like it was some sort of special thing that he made just for himself, even though I knew that wasn't the case, unless he was some sort of researcher with a lot more knowledge than he should have.

"Sorry, I didn't mean to sound offensive. There's just so much going on in my life right now, and I want to get it sorted out as soon as possible. I'm sure you can understand me." I brushed my fingers through my hair, stepping away from him. He was so close to me that he was overwhelming me, which was something I didn't expect this morning.

I realized that spending any more time here was a mistake, and thus was planning on making it so my stay here was going to be brief.

"It's okay. I can certainly understand what you are going through, which is why I'm going to help you some more. I can give you a ride to the City Hall."

I smiled hesitantly. Even though his help was something I needed, I was pretty well aware of the dangers that would come with it.

And after going through so much with Forger, I didn't think I was ready to spend any more time with another biker, even though Razor was so hot that he was almost melting my panties.

Even breathing was difficult now.

"Cat got your tongue?" He asked, chuckling. He could see how much I was struggling with this, and he was taking advantage of that. He was even finding it funny.

I shook my head, trying to bring myself back to reality. I wasn't going to make a fool of myself, even though that was already happening and I couldn't do anything against it.

"No, it's nothing like that. Just trying to make sure I'm saying the right words."

And when he was going to open his mouth again, I heard a pair of footsteps coming toward us. I turned my eyes to where they were coming from, finding none other than Forger.

He glanced at his buddy and when I thought I was going to see sparks of lightning flying between them, they both smiled.

It was the kind of smile that showed me that they were friends and that they felt good when they were together.

"I see you've met my new friend, Razor," Forger said, stopping when he was with us. Now that I had these two bikers surrounding me, I felt even smaller and shorter than I was, which was certainly something that didn't happen often. I was a bigger girl, after all.

"She's very nice, except for the fact that she was about to leave without saying goodbye. I don't know about you, but I think that's rude."

"I think the same way," Forger lamented, turning his face toward me. "And don't you think you should do something about that?"

Even though it was a question, I knew that he wasn't interested in the answer. Rather, he was using it to control and 'guide' me, and I wasn't sure for how much longer I could keep pretending that their intimidating nature wasn't affecting me. In fact, it was the opposite. It was melting my resolve second after second.

"I don't know…"

"How about going back into the club with us?" Forger asked, putting his hand on my shoulder and then leading me back inside. Even though he wasn't forcing me to do that, I felt compelled to. The truth was that it was already a long while since someone was doing what they were doing to me. I felt that they had a crush on me, and I was excited about it. The last time that happened, I didn't know what I was doing and it ended up that I didn't lose my virginity, which was something I was ashamed of.

And no way I was going to say anything about that to them. If this was going to lead to something else, then I didn't want them to be disappointed. I was pretty sure that bikers like them were used to experienced women, and I wasn't one of those.

Nothing else needed to be said. They knew that they had a

huge crush on me, that I thought that they were hot, and it was finally time to let some of that out. So much so that when we went back to the second floor and I found myself in their room, I wasn't ashamed of what was happening.

"Do you want something so that we can better talk about what's going on?" Razor asked, chuckling right after. He was finding this whole situation funny and I, in turn, was finding it embarrassing.

I shook my head, heat rising to my cheeks. There was nothing else that needed to be said. They were going to fuck me and I was going to lose my virginity. Even though I was being blunt about it, I just needed it to be done.

So much so that I wasn't surprised when Forger stepped so that he was behind me, putting his hand under my shirt and then lifting it.

"You are so quiet again, and I don't like it," he murmured against my neck, putting his hands on my waist and then applying pressure with them softly, moving his fingers against my skin. I could feel how calloused his hands were, and it was certainly hot.

"I have to tell you something," I said and then he put his hand on my mouth, closing it. I knew that he was going to do it, but I was still slightly surprised.

"You don't have to tell us anything. We know that you went through a lot and that you need to let some of it out," he murmured against my neck, pecking it with his lips. The way he did that sent shivers down my spine, and it was like he was everywhere in me.

My panties were melting even though we weren't doing anything special, which I thought was going to happen.

"Do you want me to go on?" He asked, kissing my shoulder once and then one more time, the way he was doing that passionate and slow. He was so romantic and I thought he would never be like that.

I nodded. There was no point in pretending that I shouldn't be doing this.

"Good. I knew that you were going to give us the right answer,"

Razor said, stepping toward me and then taking me to the bed, where he made me lie down on it.

Now that I was lying down on it, I felt exposed. And I felt even more so when he put his fingers under my skirt, lowering it.

I knew he was going to do that, but I was still surprised when he did it. I felt his fingers moving against my skin as he did that, sending shockwaves of pleasure across it.

I knew how this morning was going to end, and I was expecting every second of it.

CHAPTER 4

When he finished lowering my skirt, it was like he was making me feel everything that I was feeling on purpose, even though that couldn't be possible. He had a dirty smile on his face and it was showing how overconfident he was.

I didn't know if he was suspecting that I was a virgin, but he was aware that I was inexperienced. He wouldn't be acting this way if he didn't think that about me.

I felt shivers going down my spine again. It was one thing to be hoping that we were going to have sex and another for that to be happening this way. I was so inexperienced that I just didn't know what I should be doing.

"I should go for it first," Razor murmured, lowering his head and brushing his finger over my toes. I had no idea if he had a thing for feet, but what he was doing was certainly hot.

He was doing it slowly, taking his time, all the while keeping his hands on my legs.

I thought that what he was doing was already overwhelming enough, but then I realized that it wasn't even the tip of the iceberg. Forger climbed onto the bed and brushed his finger across my left nipple, making my body shudder. I knew that it was going to give me immense pleasure, but it was still too overwhelming.

He noticed that, lifting his head back up.

"Are you feeling okay, Buttercup?" Forger asked, smiling devilishly. He was always so overconfident and even though that should be pissing me off, it was making me feel the opposite. It wasn't that I was falling in love with him, but that I just wanted to continue our sex, and I knew he thought the same.

He brushed his hand over my belly, rubbing his finger in my belly button.

"Your skin is so smooth," he murmured against my ear, putting his tongue out and then flicking it on my earlobe. I closed my eyes, feeling my orgasm growing and rising in my body. I knew that when it came out, it would wash over me, and I was already waiting for that.

I knew that it would be the best orgasm of my life, and I couldn't wait for it.

"You should tell me if and when you want me to stop," Razor said, putting my toes in his mouth, and then I felt his tongue brushing over them, and doing other things with them that were difficult to put into words.

Whatever it was that he was doing, it was working. I could feel the temperature of my body rising, breathing was becoming increasingly more difficult, and I could feel sweat coming out of my pores.

"I will," I croaked and it felt like the most difficult thing I said in my life. And yet, I felt that even if it came to that, I just wouldn't be able to say the right words when they were needed.

All I knew was that his finger rubbing my belly button was driving me wild, and that wasn't even the beginning of this. He showed me that when he moved his finger back up, putting it on my lip and then making me suck it. It was actually... Oddly delicious, which was something I never thought I would say about it.

"You like this, don't you?" He murmured to me and there was no point in lying about it. I just nodded, giving the answer he was looking for. Forger smiled and kissed my neck again, letting his lips linger there for moments longer than they needed to.

The way he was doing it was so delicious that shockwaves of pleasure were traversing my body. The longer it went on, the closer I felt to reaching my climax, and I knew that it was going to strike me hard.

"Good, because there's so much more than that," he said again and I knew that it was a promise. It didn't matter what was going to happen now, he was going to bring me so much pleasure that I was going to get addicted to it.

And I just remembered that Razor was in front of my pussy. Well, not exactly in front of it, to be more precise. My panties were still protecting it from him, and I knew he was eyeing them. And thus, I wasn't surprised when he lowered my panties, exposing me to his wrath.

My body was trembling, but I was still so addicted to what was happening I wasn't even thinking about stopping any of this. It wasn't like we even agreed on a safeword or anything of the sort, after all. If and when I was in peril, I would be screwed.

"I love this part so much," Razor whispered more to himself than to me, lowering my panties and exposing my bottom parts. I knew what was going to happen, and yet I was still surprised when he started to lick at my sex, making me feel quick shock-waves of pleasure through my body. They were brief, but utterly powerful and destructive.

When he stopped doing that, I looked down and found his eyes. They were staring right at me and the smirk on his face told me everything he was thinking. He was going to be the one to take my V-card and when he was deep inside of me, he would remind me of that. He would claim me so hard it would be difficult for me to ever go back to my normal self.

"Please..." I begged, the word itself feeling so difficult to pronounce. It was like I was hurting my throat with needles.

I could see the glint of my wetness on his tongue, and noticing that was turning me on more than I already was. I knew I was going to see that, but my eyes were still surprised.

"Please, what?" He asked and it was then I knew that there was no point going on any further with whatever I thought I was saying.

Razor had his attention focused on just one thing, and that was my sex. When he was inside of it, he would be coming in there, and there would be nothing I would be able to do against that.

I didn't say anything. There was no point in replying to him and he knew that.

It was for that reason he widened his smile, lowering his head one more time before giving my snatch long, controlled licks. The way he was doing that was unbelievably wonderful, making me feel so much pleasure I feared it was going to make me pass out.

But thankfully, one more thing was keeping me here, and that was Forger doing everything he could with the other part of me.

"Hate to say it, but I love it when you are so quiet. I love it when you are always so submissive," he said, pecking my skin and then flicking his tongue over my nipple, making my body go wild. I was trembling and sweating so much that I thought I would never return to normal.

And we weren't even doing anything special yet. There was still so much to happen.

"Love your nipples so much, too," Forger whispered again, easing it inside his mouth and working on it for what felt like hours. My breathing was quickening, the pleasure was overflowing from me, and I was already sweating coldly.

Realizing just how difficult this was being to me, he let my nipple slip out of his mouth, smiling softly as I noticed that my wetness was on his lips too.

I feared he wasn't going to like that, but he was showing me that he was feeling the opposite of that. He was very much enjoying it. He enjoyed how I tasted, and knowing that, in turn, was making me feel like giving myself fully to them.

And thinking that, I just realized that I hadn't even seen their cocks in person and in all their glory. If there was something I wanted to do right now, it was that.

But I wasn't holding my breath for that. I knew that they were going to take their time and when they were ready for it, they would do it. It was for that reason that I was even managing to control my breathing, though only barely so.

"Shall we resume?" Forger asked, moving his hand around my breast and tugging on it slightly. Looking down at his crotch, I could see his dick straining against the fabric, and it was bigger than I thought. Much more so, I concluded while feeling a little afraid of it.

The worst thing that could happen now was them stopping this because they were afraid of what I was feeling.

"Yes, please," I responded and then they started to please me however they could, doing everything in their power for that. I felt a finger slipping inside my pussy, and I thought that they were finally going to take this to the next level, but then I realized that things weren't so simple.

We were going to do something different right now, and I couldn't wait for it.

CHAPTER 5

Someone grabbed my hand and pulled me so that I was on my knees on the bed. I just reopened my eyes so that I could see what was happening. I was a little taken aback by the hand yanking me suddenly, but not entirely surprised by it.

What I was surprised about was seeing them already without their pants. I thought that it was going to take them much more time to get to this point. And yet, they were so eager I couldn't even describe it.

I licked my lips. There was no denying that I was being slutty and I wasn't going to do anything to change that.

I just had to check out their cocks, finding how big they were. It was a little difficult to find out who was bigger, but there was no denying that they were both massive, veiny, and entirely everything I wanted right now.

I knew that it was going to be hard, that they were going to fuck my mouth and other holes until they were in pain, and I was still going along with it.

"Didn't think you were so hungry, Buttercup," Forger said, stepping toward me and then grabbing my hand again.

I wondered what he was going to do with it and it wasn't surprising when he put it around his dong, making me tug on the skin.

"What are you doing?" I asked, moving my eyes up and then meeting his pupils. They were regarding me attentively, which shouldn't be any different than if he was doing this with another woman.

"Since it's obvious you are a little inexperienced, I'm going to give you a hint. Or, I think I'm going to give you much more than that. I'm going to teach you how to suck someone off properly," he growled slightly, making my skin go numb. I knew that he was aware I was inexperienced, which meant that he was probably suspecting I was a virgin, too.

I gulped. If he already knew that, then it meant he was okay with it.

He pulled up the side of his lips again, smiling. With his hand still on mine, he started to move it up and down, and I could feel how massive he was. He was so massive I wondered how he could even fit inside of me, when we got to that point.

My skin was tingling. It was the first time that something like this was happening in my life, and it was utterly thrilling.

"Can I suck you off now?" I asked sheepishly, looking like a fool. I supposed I was doing this because I wanted them to think it was going to be an unforgettable morning.

"Sure, Buttercup. You can," he replied and I closed my eyes and lowered my head. I wrapped my lips around his dickhead, feeling how hard it was. The moment when my lips were around his cockhead, I felt like I was covered by bliss. I couldn't think about anything that wasn't pleasing him in every way possible, and I was doing just that.

I knew that I couldn't go down much farther than I already was, and I wasn't going to try something so stupid.

I was going to remain where I was, just moving my mouth around his cockhead, feeling it, enjoying it, and swirling my tongue around it. I knew that he was enjoying every second of this, his moans filling the room.

And I, in turn, was also making Razor a little envious of what was happening. He wished to be part of it, which was why he climbed onto the bed, positioned himself behind me, and then slid his prick between my asscheeks.

I knew that he wasn't looking for my pussy, which was why I wasn't surprised when I felt his dickhead prodding my orifice instead.

He looked up, finding Forger's eyes. A lot of things went through that meeting of eyes, and I was pretty sure that Razor just told him he wasn't going to take my virginity. Not the one belonging to my pussy, anyway.

And knowing that was comforting and also a little frightening.

He grabbed my ass and when he realized that penetrating my orifice was going to be harder than he thought, he spat on his hand. It happened so fast that I wasn't even aware of what he was doing until it was already too late.

One moment he was with his hands on my ass and then the next he was rubbing his wet finger on my asshole and then inside it, making sure that he was wetting it properly.

It was already wet and ready for his rough, sudden entry. I couldn't wait until he was doing it, pounding in and out of me, making me feel things I never thought possible. I knew that it was going to hurt, but I was still going along with it. So much so that I started to shake my ass slightly, showing him just how willing I was.

He slapped my ass gently, and I could tell that he was smiling. I couldn't peek over my shoulder, but it was a given that he was smiling. He was always such an overconfident jerk and now was no different, after all.

"You're sluttier than I thought you were," he said, gliding his hands over my ass and then penetrating me with his cock. It finished faster than I could process how it was happening, and in no moment at all, he was deep inside of me.

I could feel his prick stretching me, widening my walls, and it was as painful as it was incredible. I groaned, shutting my eyes and then pursing my lips.

And even though the pain was everywhere in my body, I didn't ask him to stop. If anything, I begged for him to keep on going.

Forger's dick, which was inside my mouth before, wasn't there any longer. It had slipped out, and it was swinging left and right in front of my face. Now that I was already getting used to the pain, it was time to continue the blowjob that I was artfully giving him.

And I knew he was expecting that, too.

He put his hand on my head, moving it down and over my cheek. He stopped when his finger was brushing over my bottom lip and then he grabbed my chin, lifting my head slightly.

Our eyes met once more, and he spoke so many things through that stare that it was unbelievable. He made me even more frightened than I already was, and my heart was pounding in my throat.

"I want you to do something special for me," he murmured and then didn't say anything else. I was a little worried that he wasn't going to continue, but then he added, "You're going to deep-throat me."

"Are you sure I can do that? I don't know if I can…" I said sheepishly. It was one thing imagining I could deep-throat him, and another trying to do it. It was so difficult, and I just couldn't imagine myself putting all of him inside of me. It would be so hard. I knew that it would wreck my mouth, which wasn't something I was waiting for.

He smiled and his smile was devilish. I didn't expect anything different coming from him, I thought.

And then I gulped. He wanted to go and do it, and there wasn't much he could do about that. When Forger had his mind set on doing something, I could tell he was the kind of guy that didn't stop until the end.

"Yes, I know you can," he said, brushing the head of his prick over my lips, and I knew it was the cue I was waiting for. And so, without thinking about it much, I just opened my mouth as wide as I could and then I let his dick go in there, sliding between my lips.

I could feel it going down until it was lodged in my throat. I could already feel it irritating that part of me, but I still wasn't going to ask him to stop. I knew that I was probably going to start gagging too, but it was worth it.

I felt so submissive and utterly destroyed with his prick inside my mouth the way it was.

I wondered if he was going to ask if I was feeling okay with this, but he kept his lips sealed. And then, he started to roll his hips at the same moment that Razor began to do the same.

If I thought before that the pain was everywhere in my body, now it was like needles were piercing my skin. It was difficult to even imagine what my body was like before this.

And in the end, I was just waiting until they were coming inside of my cunt. When that was happening, I knew I would finally feel complete.

CHAPTER 6

What was happening before didn't stop, and actually it only got worse for me. I could feel I was going to begin gagging and I wasn't doing anything to stop it. My orifice was in much more pain than it had ever been, and it was absolutely addictive. I couldn't even consider stopping what was in course, and I was pretty sure that Forger and Razor thought the same.

I was glad I was thanking them for all their help. They thought I was being rude when I was going to walk out of here without doing that, and now I was making up for it.

"God, you're so lovely when you're moaning like this," Razor said, his pace still frenetic. I didn't think he was going to slow down anytime soon, which was certainly something that I found utterly positive.

I just could feel his prick doing so much against my ass, and then there were also his balls slapping against it, which was even more pleasing than what his dick was doing.

Never before did I feel so much bliss in my life, and I knew that they were aware of that. It was for that reason that Forger and Razor were already probably planning on making me theirs for the rest of my life, too.

Forger's rod kept on sliding in and out of my mouth forcedly, hitting the back of my throat. He wasn't even ashamed of what he was doing and, in fact, it was empowering him. I could feel his balls getting hotter as time passed, and I wondered what it would be like when he was unloading his come in there.

I knew that it would be amazing.

I wasn't even doing anything other than moaning, groaning, and huffing. Breathing was so difficult I was almost feeling like I was running out of air, even though that wasn't the case.

There was more air than we needed here in the room. It was just that our sex was entirely taxing, and the bikers were aware of that.

"I think it's about time we finally did what she's looking for," Forger suggested, looking up and finding Razor's eyes. The latter nodded, and I didn't know what it was that they were talking about. But that lasted no more than a couple of seconds, for I soon figured it out.

They were talking about taking my virginity, and my mind was already going nuts.

The gleam of happiness in my eyes was telling of that. So much so that Forger was excitedly happy about it, pulling it out of my mouth a moment later.

It was a little messy when he did that, sloppy even, but his dick was already hard and ready to penetrate my pussy.

The only problem with that was that I didn't think they were willing to choose who should take my virginity first. There was going to be a little fight about that, and I didn't even like thinking about it. I just wanted both of them to be happy when they shared me that way.

Razor pulled out of me as well, climbing off the bed.

"I think I should be the first," he suggested, and then Forger put his hand on his chest, stopping him.

Their eyes met, narrowed, and I wondered if they were going to start a battle where they punched and kicked each other right in the middle of our sex. I just didn't want that to happen, and I was afraid of it.

"I have a better solution," Forger said.

"And what solution is that?" Razor asked, even though I could tell that he already knew the answer to his question.

"The blindfold, so that Arleen doesn't know who did it," he suggested and I knew that they really were going to do it. It wasn't even something that they were going to discuss, and I was excitedly happy about it.

"Perfect. I was thinking about that, too," Razor said, opening a drawer and picking it up. He was holding it in his hand when he proceeded to me and he didn't even look at my eyes as he put the blindfold around them.

He knew that I wanted things to be happening this way, and he was just waiting until he was the one sliding his prick into my sex.

"And how are you going to decide who should do it first?" I asked and then he massaged my right cheek with his hand, taking his time.

I feared that he wasn't going to answer my question, and then he groaned slightly, most likely showing me that he wished he didn't have to share me.

"You don't need to know anything about that," he replied, and then he walked back to where Forger was.

I couldn't even hear what they were doing, my heart pounding in my head.

And then, when they decided who should do it first, I felt a pair of hands grabbing my thighs and pulling me to the man who owned them. Finding out who that was just by the way his hands felt was impossible, I thought. Their hands were too similar, after all.

I could hear his breathing, and it was ragged.

He didn't say anything, because of course he wasn't going to. He didn't want to give away his identity, which was something I was expecting. Another thing that I was expecting was when I felt his prick prodding my pussy, and it was making me arch my back.

My body was trembling, shaking, and it wasn't even the start of this. When he was inside of me, pounding in and out of me, I would be utterly devastated. I didn't think I would ever be able to go back to my normal self.

I felt his hands moving around me, feeling every part of me. He even pinched my right nipple, moving his hand around my breast.

He was feeling it, kneading it, and also massaging it. It was almost like he was taking his time, which was something I expected from him, whoever he was.

I felt that, when he was inside of me, when his prick was stretching my walls, even then I wouldn't be able to find out who he was. His identity was hidden from me, and that was torture in and of itself.

With a little thrust of his hips, he went inside of me and broke through the initial barrier. I felt it stretching my walls and then the pain was shooting in every part of my body. I bit my bottom lip, and then I tried to scream, but then I felt a hand closing my mouth.

I didn't know whose hand that was, just that I didn't expect it. He didn't want me to scream, most likely so that the other bikers didn't hear it. I was pretty sure that they were thinking that they didn't want anyone else to find out about what we were doing. It wasn't that they were ashamed of it, but that it was our dirty, little secret.

And then I heard him whispering into my ear, probably with his finger between his lips. He was asking me to keep my mouth shut, and I was certainly going to do it. The last thing I wanted right now was to do anything that could piss him off.

The dick that was already inside of me continued to cover more distance, going all the way to the end. And then when he met another resistance, he just went through it like it was nothing.

I knew that it was my hymen and that it was no more. I finally lost my virginity, and my body was shaking in response.

I just finally hit my climax and it was the most exhilarating thing that ever happened in my life. It wasn't the first-ever climax of my life, but it was powerful and it was making my body shake uncontrollably. I even thought I was going to pass out, but then I felt the lips of the guy that was by my side kissing me.

He was assuring me that everything was going to be fine and that he wanted me awake. After all, he was the second one that was going to start ramming it in and out of me, and it was going to be the most amazing thing that ever happened after my first fuck with the other biker.

Minutes later, the first biker that was destroying my cunt pulled out and then moved away. I didn't know what he was going to do, but then the second biker eased his dick in there, rolling his hips right away, and then I stopped wondering about that.

His pace was frenetic from the get-go and even though I was feeling a lot of pain, I matched him thrust for thrust. I didn't think I was going to be able to do that, but it was happening, and it was so good that I couldn't stop it.

And then my orgasm washed over me for the second time, and I was breathing so hard and everything I was doing felt so painful I just couldn't go on any longer.

I didn't pass out, but I still collapsed on the bed.

And when I thought that someone was going to put his arms around me and tell me that everything was going to be okay, they put their clothes back on and left me unattended. I was a little pissed off at that, but it wasn't unexpected.

They were bikers, after all.

EPILOGUE

But they didn't leave me alone for too long. After having such an amazing morning with them, I decided that I needed something else. I wasn't going to start my life over somewhere else, with other people, and with conditions completely different from the ones I ended up choosing. In fact, I decided that the right choice was living with the bikers for the rest of my life, and I was doing that.

I was doing that with a smile on my face.

I was in the backseat of the motorcycle, my arms around Forger's massive and powerful body. Even though he was wearing his leather jacket, I could feel his muscles through it, and they were as hard as they had ever been.

He always worked out, always gave his all at the gym, and it couldn't be any different. When it was about taking care of his body, he never half-assed it.

He peeked over his shoulder. He was riding on his motorcycle and we had no particular destination. He was taking me somewhere and we didn't even know where that was. I just could feel the wind blowing against my face, throwing up my hair, and the heat of the sun on my back.

Razor was with us, riding on his motorcycle. I would be riding on it pretty soon, about a couple of hours from now, to be more precise. Even though Forger and Razor were friends, they were possessive of me.

They didn't like sharing me much, even though they couldn't do much about that. Without sharing me, things would get out of hand.

And they were aware of that. So much so that no fight broke out between them yet, and I was happy for that.

"Everything okay with you?" Forger asked, smiling. He didn't wear his helmet, even though he should. I always nagged him about it, and maybe one day I would be able to change his mind. I loved him.

There was no denying it and I wanted to make sure that he was always safe, even though that was something that was never part of a biker's life. I just sighed, thinking about that.

Forger was always so stubborn, and it was annoying.

"Yes, everything is okay with me," I replied, nodding. It was enough to rest his mind about it, and then he thrust his foot against the pedal of the motorcycle, propelling it forward even faster than it was already going.

If I thought before the wind was already too strong against my face, now it was even more so. I felt like it was going to blow me off the motorcycle, which of course didn't happen. As long as I was with Forger, everything was going to be fine.

And I wouldn't have it any other way.

A moment later, we pulled over by a hill overlooking the city. Seeing it from over here was fascinating and so perfect that I couldn't imagine myself doing anything different.

I got off the bike and Forger put his arm around me in a way that told me that I was his property.

And I was okay with that. I was also okay with being Razor's property, and he was even smiling at that, even though he wasn't completely fine with not having his arm around me. He was going to do that as soon as the opportunity presented itself, I thought amusingly.

We were standing by the edge of the hill, overlooking the city when Forger said, "It's really beautiful. When I think about retiring and living the rest of my life with someone, and that someone being you, I want to do it here. I grew up in the city, and it's my home."

He looked down, dipping his head before kissing me. The kiss was electric and passionate, and I was loving it.

And just to make sure that Razor wasn't going to feel any more envious than he already was, I snapped my head to the right and kissed him as well.

He wanted to make up for the time that he wasn't all over me, the kiss being so passionate I thought that he was going to start using his tongue as well. But that didn't happen, especially because he didn't want to piss off his friend, and that was something I could respect about him.

I put my arm around his waist, feeling the muscles and how hard and warm they were. They were so hard that I was pretty sure he had almost no body fat, which was a big achievement. It was certainly something I would never be able to achieve as well.

Everything was fine, the sun was setting in the distance, and my life with them was going to be picture-perfect. I never thought that I would end up with two bikers, but here I was…

The End

Read the first book of the series here:

1. Dirty Doctors: Steamy BWWM Mafia

Or you can also read a sneak peek of this story on the next page.

Lastly, leave your review. I love reading your feedback!

TEASER: DIRTY DOCTORS

Series: Plus Size - 1

I wiped the sweat off my forehead, thinking that things couldn't be getting any worse for me even if I tried to. I was in front of the car and then I popped up the engine's lid, coughing when smoke hit my face. It smelled pretty bad and it was dark, reminding me that whatever was going on here, it wasn't good for me, especially given that I wanted to get to the airport as soon as possible. I had a trip planned to go to Italy, where I was going to spend my well-earned vacation.

It was dark and the moon was high in the sky. It was a full moon, which was extremely bright. My eyes couldn't spot many clouds in the sky, something that I didn't think much of. The stars twinkled in the deadness of the night, making me feel that they were pretty much part of the only thing keeping me company here.

My car wasn't old, but it wasn't a top model either. So much so that it wasn't surprising that it broke down on me right when I was still traveling in and crossing the countryside.

Where I was, I couldn't even see the nearest city, which was saying something. The state where I was didn't have much in terms of the countryside. Some farms populated the region, but they weren't part of the dominating presence. That was, of course, the cities and the villages.

I shook my head and started to go to the right of the car when my eyes spotted two glowing orbs in the distance. For a moment, I didn't think much of them, overlooking them when the following thought crossed my mind - even though I was pretty much alone here and didn't think that anyone was going to come this way, it was possible I got lucky this time.

I waved my arms over my head, hoping that they were going to notice that I was stranded on the road. It was a dirt road, so it wasn't surprising when they shot past me in their car that dust and dirt were kicked up by their tires, making me cough again.

I waved my hands in front of my face, stepping away from the smoke of those things that they must have generated on purpose. I thought for a moment that they weren't going to stop, but a smile crept up on my face when I noticed that I was wrong.

The red lights of their car grew in intensity as they pulled back, stopping by my side. I peered inside the vehicle as I noticed that it really was two men driving their Mustang. I didn't think much of it, but soon I realized that they were hot and burly.

I took a second to dissect them with my eyes. My eyes went up and down slowly, carefully analyzing who they appeared to be. I was just a little paranoid that they were criminals. Given the high-class look on their faces, I didn't think that they were, but I couldn't be sure, either.

What I was sure about was that they were my type. So much so that my nipples were getting slightly hard, which was something that didn't happen often anymore these days. One of the reasons for that was that after realizing that my crush didn't want any-thing to do with me, I lost any and all interest I had in love. It faded out of my mind and I didn't think it would ever come back.

They didn't have much in terms of clothes, opting for plain shirts, jean shorts, dark shoes, and not much more than that. I no-ticed that one of the guys had short, dark hair and that the other had slightly longer hair, but that it was blond.

They both had some scruff on their faces, suggesting that they hadn't shaved in a while. I wondered if that meant they had been on the road for some time already, but I didn't think that it was prudent of me to ask them about that.

I decided not to. After all, my mind was more preoccupied with other things.

The one that was sitting closest to me analyzed me with his eyes, smiling softly. I had no idea what that meant, but I was beginning to grow a little more suspicious of what it could be.

I didn't want to think that he harbored dirty, secret thoughts regarding me, but that appeared to be the case.

I could see the glint of the color of his eyes. They were the same color as jade, which was so pretty that it made me want to do things with him that, otherwise, I wouldn't even be thinking about right now.

It wasn't just that my nipples were hard right now, but that they were like little pebbles on my breasts.

"Need a little help with something, miss?" He asked, opening the door of his car and then stepping out alongside his friend. When they shut the door of their cars, I noticed how tall they were. They were much taller than me, which was one other thing that made them the eye candies they were.

They tipped up their chins, looking more confident. I certainly didn't think that I was going to find myself in the presence of such burly, confident men, but here I was. They were so imposing that they made me feel smaller than I was, which wasn't something that happened often.

After all, I was a plus-size girl with plenty of curves. Perhaps that was something that they found attractive about me, which was a possibility. The way that their eyes were scanning me told me that, too. I stepped away from them, but then my butt touched the frame of the car. I knew that I had nowhere to escape to, not that I was thinking about doing that, though...

MORE BOOKS LIKE THIS ONE

SERIES - FIRST TIME QUICKIES

They compete over her, want every part of her, and nothing can stop them.

1. Claiming her Age Gap: Reverse Harem Mafia

2. Selling her Age Gap: Reverse Harem Mafia

3. Loving her Age Gap: Reverse Harem Mafia

Or download all the books in this convenient, cheap bundle:

1. Our Princess: Mafia Reverse Harem Bundle

SERIES - IN PUBLIC

It's all about doing it in public, shamelessly, and dominating their exposed princesses.

1. Fed from Behind: Rear Entrance Devoured by Multiple Men

2. Fed from Behind: Tight Squeeze by Multiple Men

3. Fed from Behind: Taken by Multiple Men on Christmas Day

4. Fed from Behind: Tight Squeeze in front of the Christmas Tree

5. Tight Squeeze: Petite for Big Alpha Men of the House

ABOUT THE AUTHOR

Leandra Camilli's obsession? Writing dirty, steamy stories that make her readers drool. She loves her Alpha males, hucows, sissies, and futas. If you're searching for those kinds of books, look no further.

With a cup of coffee on her table and warm socks on, she writes almost every day. Leandra Camilli has featured in several top 100 categories in the store, and she publishes weekly.